For Jackie Kerin, who wished out loud that someone would write a fishy tale – CS

To the ever-supportive, most amazing parents in the world, Anne and Gordon,
and to my beau beau beau Bruno the Brave, thank you – CA

This edition published by Kids Can Press in 2014

Text © 2010 Claire Saxby
Illustrations © 2010 Cassandra Allen

Published in arrangement with Walker Books Australia Pty. Ltd.

Kids Can Press acknowledges the financial support of the Government of Ontario, through the Ontario Media Development Corporation's Ontario Book Initiative.

Published in Canada by
Kids Can Press Ltd.
25 Dockside Drive
Toronto, ON M5A 0B5

Published in the U.S. by
Kids Can Press Ltd.
2250 Military Road
Tonawanda, NY 14150

www.kidscanpress.com

The artwork in this book was rendered in gouache and pencil.
The text is set in Poliphilus MT.

Edited by Virginia Grant
Designed by Miriam Steenhauer

This book is smyth sewn casebound.
Manufactured by Leo Paper Products, in 10/2013

CM 14 0 9 8 7 6 5 4 3 2 1

LIBRARY AND ARCHIVES CANADA CATALOGUING IN PUBLICATION

Saxby, Claire, author
There was an old sailor / written by Claire Saxby ; illustrated by Cassandra Allen.

Originally published: Sydney : Walker Books and subsidiaries, 2010.
For children aged 3–7.

ISBN 978-1-77138-022-5 (bound)

I. Allen, Cassandra, illustrator II. Title.

PZ7.S257T54 2014   j823'.914   C2013-903140-5

Kids Can Press is a CORUS™ Entertainment company

There Was an Old Sailor

CLAIRE SAXBY ⚓ CASSANDRA ALLEN

There was an old sailor ...

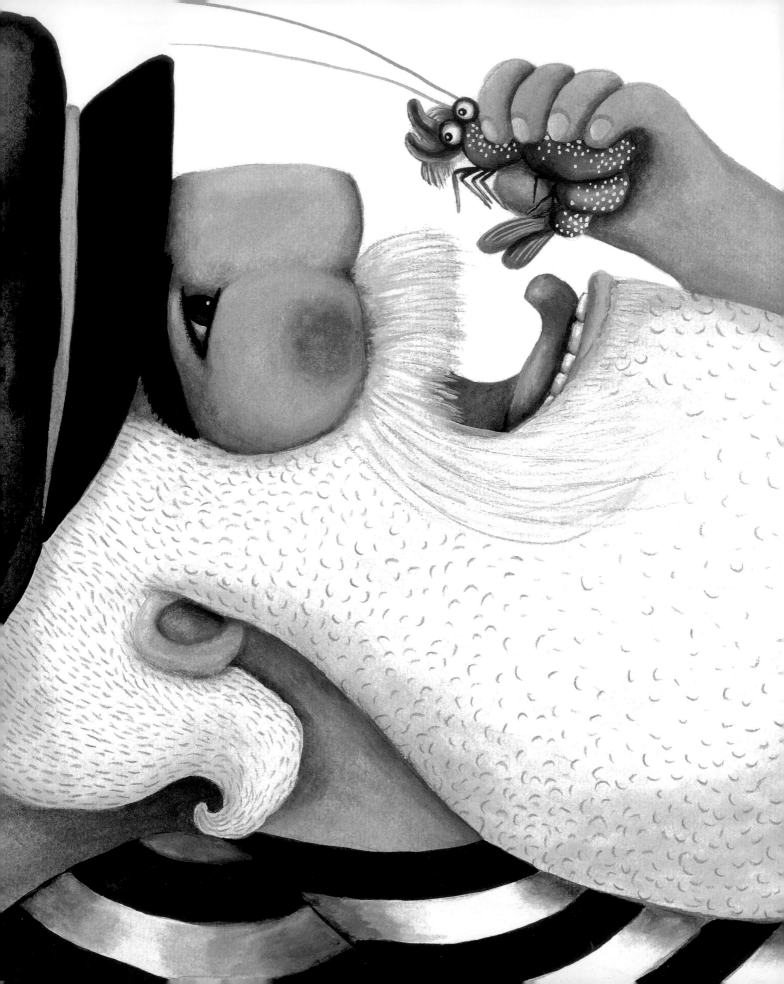

who swallowed a krill.

I don't know why
he swallowed the krill —

It'll make him ill.

There was an old sailor
who swallowed a jelly

That wriggled and wriggled
and jiggled his belly.

He swallowed the jelly
to catch the krill.

I don't know why
he swallowed the krill —

It'll make him ill.

There was an old sailor
who swallowed a fish.

With a wish and a swish
he swallowed the fish!

He swallowed the fish
to catch the jelly

That wriggled and wriggled
and jiggled his belly.

He swallowed the jelly
to catch the krill.

I don't know why
he swallowed the krill —

It'll make him ill.

There was an old sailor
who swallowed a squid.

Yes, he did —
he swallowed a squid!

He swallowed the squid
to catch the fish.

He swallowed the fish
to catch the jelly

That wriggled and wriggled
and jiggled his belly.

He swallowed the jelly
to catch the krill.

I don't know why
he swallowed the krill —

It'll make him ill.

There was an old sailor
who swallowed a ray.

Oh, what a day when
he swallowed the ray!

He swallowed the ray
to catch the squid.

He swallowed the squid
to catch the fish.

He swallowed the fish
to catch the jelly

That wriggled and wriggled
and jiggled his belly.

He swallowed the jelly
to catch the krill.

I don't know why
he swallowed the krill —

It'll make him ill.

There was an old sailor
who swallowed a seal.

He had to kneel
to swallow the seal!

He swallowed the seal
to catch the ray.

He swallowed the ray
to catch the squid.

He swallowed the squid
to catch the fish.

He swallowed the fish
to catch the jelly

That wriggled and wriggled
and jiggled his belly.

He swallowed the jelly
to catch the krill.

I don't know why
he swallowed the krill —

It'll make him ill.

There was an old sailor
who swallowed a shark.

It must have been dark
when he swallowed the shark!

He swallowed the shark
to catch the seal.

He swallowed the seal
to catch the ray.

He swallowed the ray
to catch the squid.

He swallowed the squid
to catch the fish.

He swallowed the fish
to catch the jelly

That wriggled and wriggled
and jiggled his belly.

He swallowed the jelly
to catch the krill.

I don't know why
he swallowed the krill —

It'll make him ill.

There was an old sailor
who swallowed a whale …

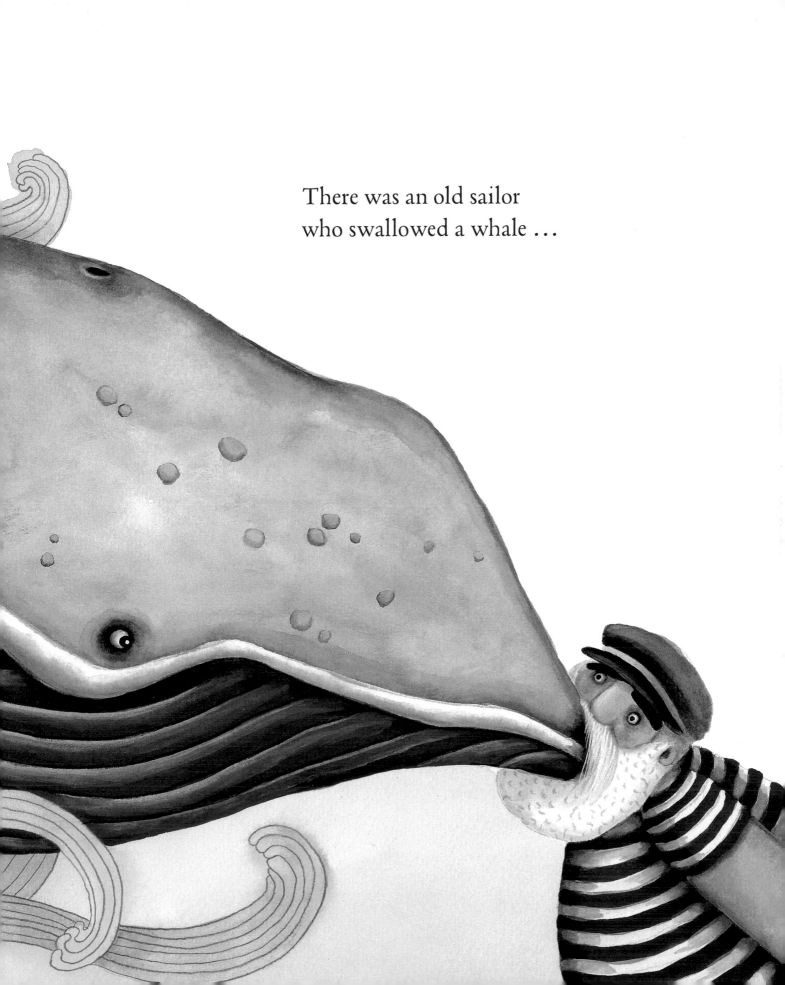

then with a burp …

set sail.

Fishy Facts

Krill are tiny critters. Five krill weigh about the same as one teaspoon of sugar!

Jellyfish catch their food using tiny stinging threads like miniature harpoons. Ka-zing!

There is no such thing as a fish finger. Fish only have fins.

A blue whale can eat millions of krill a day!

A squid has a strong beak – like a parrot – to catch crabs and chomp fish.

With eyes on top and a mouth underneath, a ray must be very careful at dinnertime.

Seals have sensitive whiskers to help them find their favorite foods. Some even have beards.

Sharks will never need false teeth. They grow new teeth whenever they lose any.